Little Evie
in the
Wild Wood

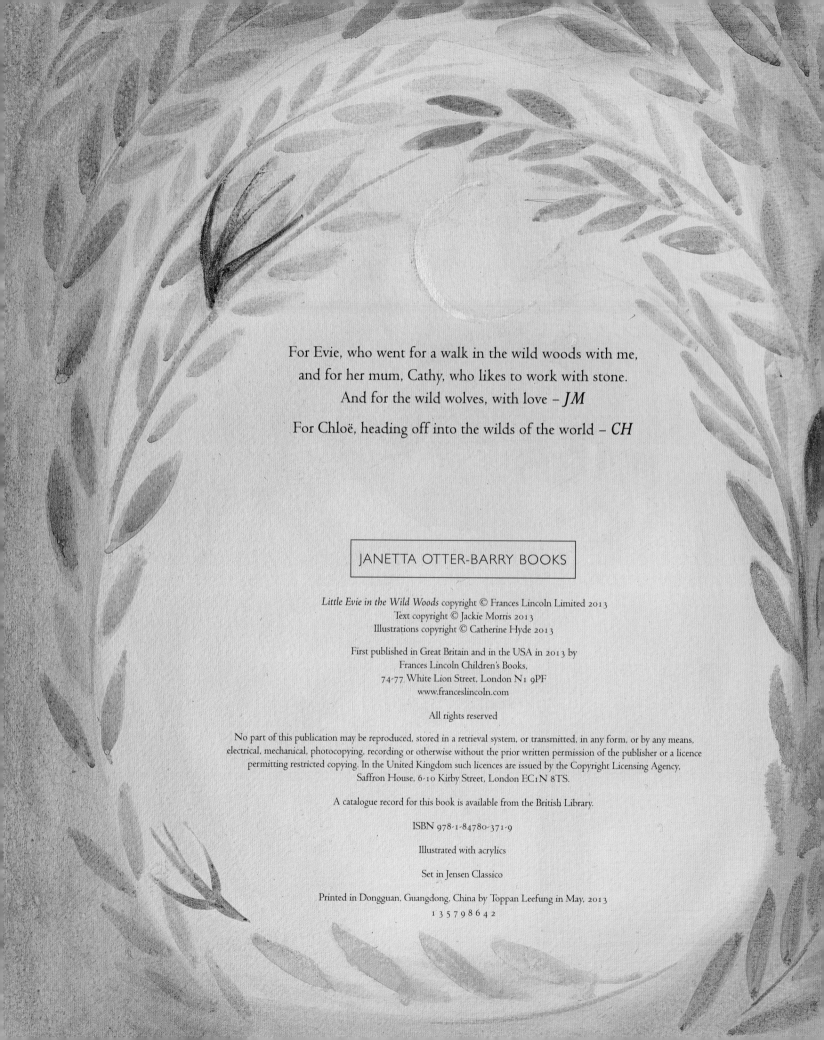

For Evie, who went for a walk in the wild woods with me,
and for her mum, Cathy, who likes to work with stone.
And for the wild wolves, with love – *JM*

For Chloë, heading off into the wilds of the world – *CH*

JANETTA OTTER-BARRY BOOKS

Little Evie in the Wild Woods copyright © Frances Lincoln Limited 2013
Text copyright © Jackie Morris 2013
Illustrations copyright © Catherine Hyde 2013

First published in Great Britain and in the USA in 2013 by
Frances Lincoln Children's Books,
74-77 White Lion Street, London N1 9PF
www.franceslincoln.com

A catalogue record for this book is available from the British Library.

ISBN 978-1-84780-371-9

Illustrated with acrylics

Set in Jensen Classico

Printed in Dongguan, Guangdong, China by Toppan Leefung in May, 2013
1 3 5 7 9 8 6 4 2

Little Evie
in the
Wild Wood

Written by Jackie Morris

Illustrated by Catherine Hyde

F

FRANCES LINCOLN
CHILDREN'S BOOKS

Little Evie
stepped over the stile
and into the wild wood.
She followed the pathway
her mama had shown her
when she was young.

It was cool in the wood.
The pathway was clear.
She could smell the damp ground
where her feet disturbed
leaves that had
fallen
to earth.
The trees made a tunnel
to show Evie the way.

In patches of sunlight
          butterfly wings
    brushed her face.
Up they flew,
          towards the emerald light
               as golden leaves
          tumbled,
               turning together
    in a spiral dance.
She could hear the
               leaves
          as they
               touched
                    the earth.

Small birds chattered. Insects hummed.

The wind sang a soft song high in the tree tops.

The woodpigeons called a soft-voiced warning.

"Be careful, Evie! Be careful, Evie!"

She looked back and could just see

the bright gold of the field

in afternoon sunshine,

like a gold ring

behind her.

Deep in the wood the pathway was darker.
Little Evie felt so small
beside the ancient oak trees,
twisted by age, heavy with leaves.
She looked up and the sky was all green leaves,
a forest roof high over her head.
From deep in the wood
a fox barked a sharp call.

Her basket was heavy
and the path seemed long.
So she sat for a while,
listened to the birdsong
and the sound of the greenwood,
leaves growing, twigs cracking,
the rustle of beetles
and the buzzing of bees,
flutter of feathers.
High above the leaf roof
a mournful buzzard mewed.

Deep in the wild wood the windsong
was like the roll of the ocean.
The pathway was dappled,
dark, mysterious.

Little Evie clutched her basket tight.
She could feel eyes in the forest,
watching,
waiting. . . .

Now the pathway opened
into a clearing at the heart of the wild wood.
The sun was so bright.

Dragonflies hovered over the long grass.
At the edge of the clearing a cave,
dark as midnight.
"Excuse me," she said, voice soft as a beeswing.
"Excuse me."
No answer, but she thought she felt
a low growl
that made the earth
tremble.
Little Evie stood in the clearing.
The evening

sun

kissed

her face.

Then out
she came.

Great eyes, the better to see her with.
Great ears, the better to hear her call.
Sharp teeth like daggers,
nose black as coal.
She stood in the clearing
before Little Evie,
filling the world
with wildness.

Little Evie looked up into the amber eyes of the wolf.

"Excuse me," said Little Evie, "but Grandma sent me,

with these for you. A gift."

The wolf licked her lips.

Evie held out the basket,

and pulled back the cloth.

Shining inside

like blood-red rubies,

seven tarts with bright jam

and golden pastry.

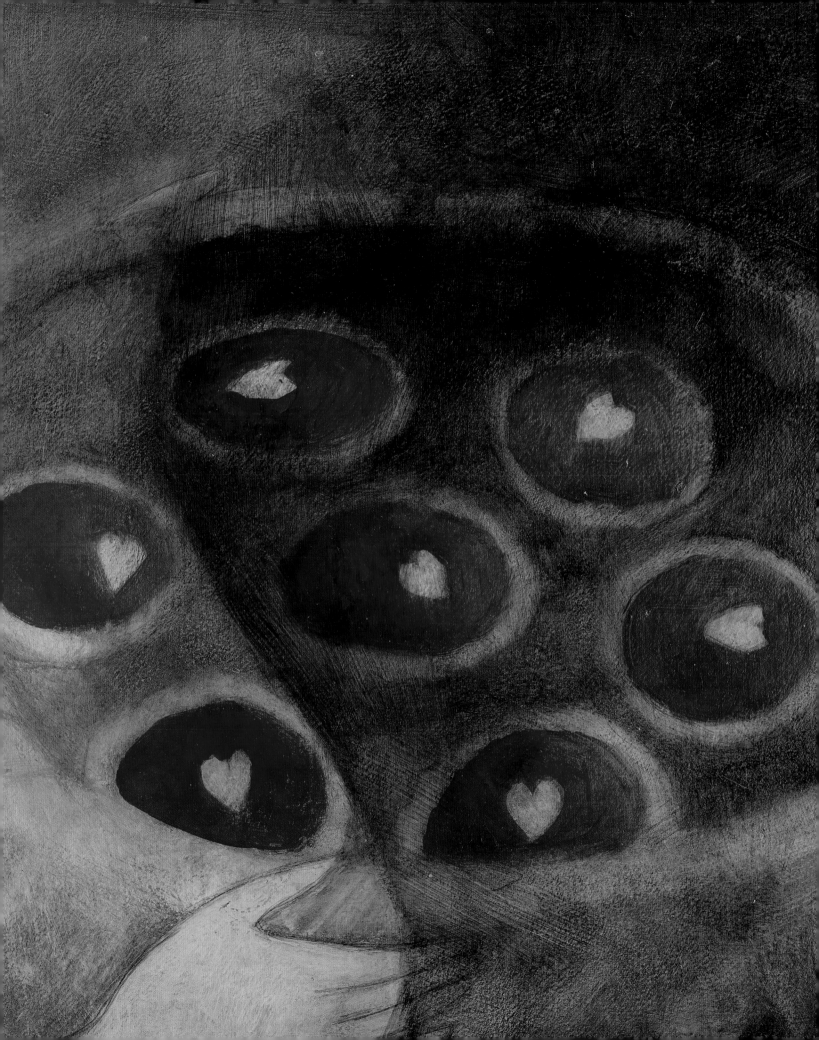

In the clearing, in the middle of the great wild wood,

the wolf and the child shared the tarts,

so warm in the evening sun, so sweet.

Little Evie stroked the wolf's velvet ears,

leant against her side, listened to her breathing.

Around them the wild wood

held its breath,

waiting.

When only golden crumbs remained
the wolf lifted the basket.
Little Evie, tired now, climbed onto her back.
The wolf was warm in the chill air of evening.
They headed back,
on the path through the wood,
a trail of birds behind
pecking golden crumbs.
Through the old wood and the twisted oaks
where the owls had begun
their evening song,
to the edge of the wild wood
where the trees
reached out into the field.

Halfway between cottage and wood
Little Evie turned. She could see the sun
setting golden, caught in the tree tops.
She could see the rising full moon
glint in the wolf's eye as she watched
from the edge.
Then she turned for home,
along the pathway so familiar, and there,
at the cottage door, was her mama,
waiting for her.

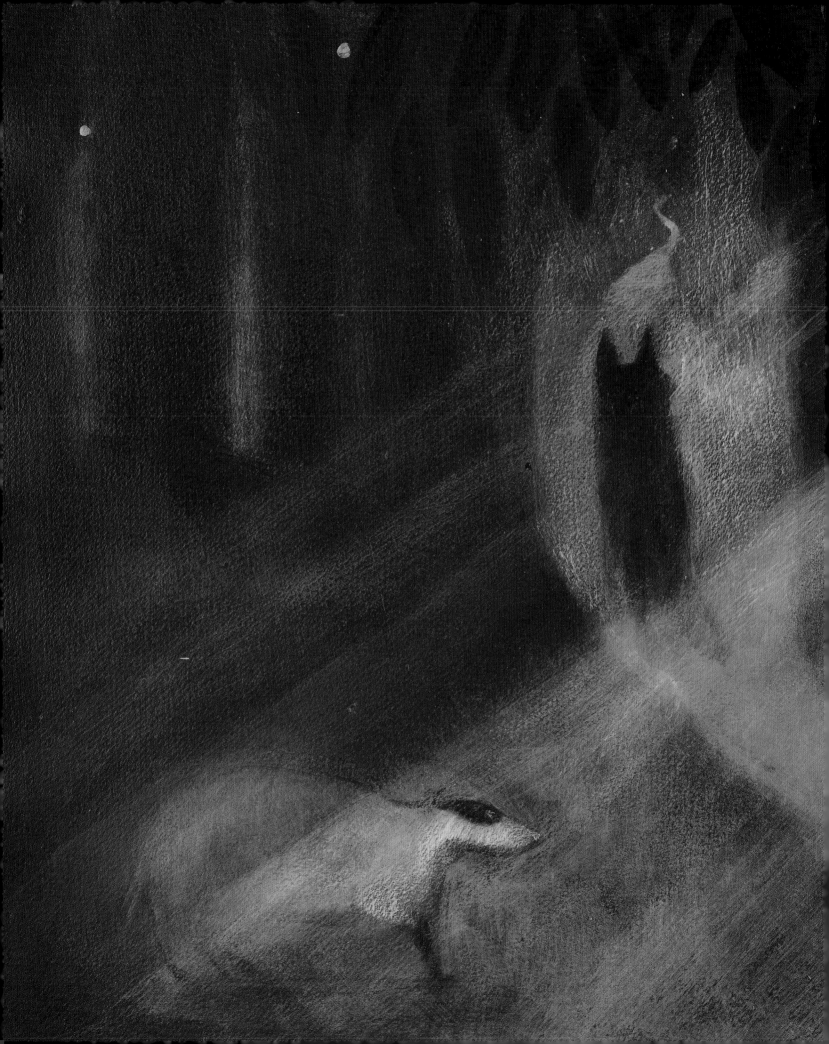